HARBINGERS

5

The Sentinels

Angela Hunt

Alton Gansky, Bill Myers,
and Frank Peretti

ANGELA HUNT

Published by Amaris Media International.

Cover Design: Angela Hunt

Photo © Layercake

ISBN: 0692380116
ISBN-13: 978-0692380116

For more information, visit us on Facebook:
https://www.facebook.com/pages/Harbingers/705107309586877
or
www.harbingersseries.com

HARBINGERS

A novella series by

Bill Myers, Frank Peretti, Angela Hunt, and Alton Gansky

In this fast-paced world with all its demands, the four of us wanted to try something new. Instead of the longer novel format, we wanted to write something equally as engaging but that could be read in one or two sittings—on the plane, waiting to pick up the kids from soccer, or as an evening's read.

We also wanted to play. As friends and seasoned novelists, we thought it would be fun to create a game we could participate in together. The rules were simple:

Rule #1

Each of us would write as if we were one of the characters in the series:

Bill Myers would write as Brenda, the street-hustling tattoo artist who sees images of the future.

Frank Peretti would write as the professor, the atheist ex-priest ruled by logic.

Angela Hunt would write as Andi, the professor's brilliant-but-geeky assistant who sees inexplicable patterns.

Alton Gansky would write as Tank, the naïve, big-hearted jock with a surprising connection to a healing power.

Rule #2

Instead of the four of us writing one novella together (we're friends but not crazy), we would write it like a TV series. There would be an overarching story line into which we'd plug our individual novellas, with each story written from our character's point of view.

Bill's first novella, *The Call*, sets the stage. It will be followed by Frank's, *The Haunted*, Angela's *The Sentinels*, and Alton's *The Girl*. And if we keep having fun, we'll begin a second round and so on until other demands pull us away or, as in TV, we get cancelled.

There you have it. We hope you'll find these as entertaining in the reading as we did in the writing.

Bill, Frank, Angie, and Al

Chapter 1

I was sitting on the edge of my grandparents' deck, bare legs swinging in the sun, when Abby trotted out of the house and sat beside me. "Abs!" I slipped my arm around her back and gave her a hug; she returned my affection by licking my cheek. "Stop that, silly. You know I'm ticklish."

As if she understood, Abby straightened and joined me in staring at the sea oats and the white sandy beaches of the Gulf of Mexico. We had sat in this same spot hundreds of times in our growing-up years . . . me, the geeky high-schooler, and Abby, the ungainly Labrador pup. Somehow we had both outgrown our awkwardness.

I ran my hand over the back of her head, then scratched between her ears. My heart welled with nostalgia as tears stung my eyes. "I've missed you, Abs," I whispered. "All that time away at college . . . I wish you could have been with me. Maybe I wouldn't have been so homesick if you were there."

She whimpered in commiseration, then gave me another kiss.

My throat tightened at the thought of eventually losing her. Big dogs tend to have shorter lifespans, and all the books said Labs lived an average of twelve to fourteen years. Which meant I'd only have my girl for another five or so years . . . I had to get home more often.

Abby pricked up her ears, pulled away from me, then jogged down the deck steps.

"Abs! You know you're not supposed to go down to the beach."

When it suited her, Abby had selective hearing. She dove into the bed of sea oats. I couldn't see her in the thick undergrowth, but the tasseled heads of the stalks bent and trembled as she passed by.

"You're going to get sand spurs in your coat!"

No answer except the rustle and crunch of dry vegetation. Then a warning bark, followed by a throaty growl.

She had probably found a rat, but for some reason her growl lifted the hairs on my arm. I stood and walked to a better vantage point, hoping to spot her. "Abby!" I brightened my voice. "Want a treat? A cookie?"

Another bark, and then a sharp yelp, followed by a frenzy of rustling and crunching. Then Abby began to cry in a constant whine as she retraced her steps, moving faster this time. Had she found a snake? Venomous snakes were not common on the beach, but this was Florida . . .

I flew down the stairs, drawn by the urgency in her tone. "Abs! Come here, honey. Come on, baby, come on out."

If she'd been bitten, I had only minutes to get her to a vet. My grandparents had left a car in the garage, keys on the ring by the door . . .

Abby appeared in the pathway. She lifted her head for an instant and wriggled her nose, parsing the air for my scent. Then she ran to me, barreling into my legs and knocking me onto the sand.

"Abs?" She was on top of me, thrashing her head while she whined, and with great difficulty I managed to catch her jowls. "Abs, honey, let me look—"

My breath caught in my throat. Abby's panicked breaths fluttered over my face as I stared into what had once been gentle brown eyes but were now empty, blood-encrusted caverns.

Everything went silent within me, and I screamed.

My grandmother's expensive sofa had a flaw in its fabric, but I didn't think Safta had noticed. The tiny dotted pattern wasn't arranged in perfectly straight lines, resulting in a slight variation that must have caused a problem for the upholsterer. Then again, perhaps a machine assembled this piece, and most machines had no feelings.

Lucky machines. Apparently the deviation in this upholstery pattern had been enough to evoke a horrific nightmare in my afternoon nap. My heart pounded for ten minutes after I woke up, then I bent down and gave Abby a huge hug, relieved to find her alive and well. But the minute I put my head back on the sofa pillow, a lingering sense of dread enveloped me.

I released a pent-up sigh. I'd been at my grandparents' beach house for a full twenty-four hours, but being home hadn't helped me relax as much as I'd hoped. Being with family usually took my mind off my work, but my grandparents had taken their jet to Miami to attend a wedding, leaving me to examine patterns on the couch, watch the professor read, and suffer quiet nightmares.

"Andi?" As if he'd overheard my thoughts, the professor lowered his book and waggled a brow. "Your grandparents have anything to snack on around here?"

"I'm sure they do. Let's go to the kitchen."

I rolled off the sofa and led the way to the ultra-modern kitchen Safta rarely used. Because she and Sabba now lived alone in this big house, they tended to eat out a lot. But my grandfather liked to snack, so the pantry was usually stocked with goodies.

Like a hungry puppy, the professor followed me to the kitchen, then craned his neck forward as I opened the pantry door. "Almonds," I said, reading the labels on cans and boxes. "Matzo crackers, cheese crackers, chocolate cookies, Oreos, and pretzel sticks. Yum, and these." I reached for a bag of jalapeño chips, my personal favorite. "If you like hot and spicy—"

"I like almonds." The professor reached past me and grabbed a can from the shelf, then popped the top. Then he hopped on a barstool, picked up the book he'd been reading, and tossed a handful of nuts into his mouth.

I understood why he was hanging around—just as I understood why he'd been reading in the living room instead of the guest room. We were both still recovering from a harrowing experience in Port Avalon, and neither of us wanted to be alone.

"Nice place your grandparents have here," the professor said, his gaze moving to the wide sliding glass door with the ocean view. "Nice of them to let us hang out here for a couple of days."

"I know."

I crossed my arms and wished I could think of some way to dispel the creepy memories of Port Avalon. When I learned that the next stop on the professor's speaking circuit was the University of Tampa, I had invited my grandparents to come hear him, since they lived only a few miles away. They passed up the opportunity to hear the professor speak on the toxicity of believing in God in a post-modern culture, but insisted that the professor and I drive over to spend the next few days with them. Of course I'd said yes—how could I refuse the people who raised me?—but my dreams of lying in warm sand vanished when I woke up this morning and spotted the cloudy horizon. Rain began to fall shortly thereafter, and the day had been melancholy, wet, and dismal ever since.

The professor didn't seem to notice the weather. This morning I found him reading one of my books on chaos theory, and even though I knew I disagreed with the premise, he seemed entranced by the topic. Occasionally he snorted as he read, sometimes he laughed aloud, and more than once I watched him scribble a note in the margin. When he finished, he'd probably quiz me on the topic, asking how I could possibly believe that the laws of science and order held room for any variation or exception.

I could answer him easily enough. All I had to do was remind him about Port Avalon, where few things had operated according to natural laws.

I walked to the fridge and dug around in the produce drawer, hoping to find something crunchy. I came up with a single scrawny carrot, which I carried to the sink. I'd no sooner finished washing it when Abby ran to my side, sat politely, and looked at me, her eyes plaintively asking for a treat.

Caught by the powerful undertow of memory, I had to resist a strong impulse to bend down and kiss those beautiful brown eyes.

I looked around for the old doggie cookie jar, but Safta's counters were now clean and bare.

"What do you want, Abs?"

The dog lifted a paw, politely asking for—what?

I followed her gaze and realized she was staring at the carrot. "You want a carrot?"

She whined.

"Okay, then." I pulled a knife from the cutlery drawer, chopped off the stub, and held out the rest. "Enjoy your vegetable."

Abby took the carrot between her teeth, then stood, wagged her tail in a polite thank-you, and trotted off to enjoy her prize.

"Well-trained dog," the Professor remarked. "Probably heard the sound of the refrigerator drawer."

I shrugged. "She's always been smart. Maybe she knew that carrots were the only decent snack in the fridge."

The professor cast me a reproachful glance. "You

shouldn't indulge in anthropomorphism, Andi. Assigning human qualities to animals is the stuff of children's tales and fables."

"But you're always telling me that humans are animals," I countered. "And in your speech yesterday you pointed out that human DNA is 98 percent identical to that of a gorilla."

"Another proof of our evolutionary history," the professor answered. "But though there is very little difference between man and the primates, what little there is, is very important. Man evolved in ways the gorilla did not, in language, social and emotional development—"

At that moment Safta entered the room, her bright orange caftan billowing behind her. "You two." She shook her head. "Always debating something. Always reading, always learning. Your brains should get tired, but do they? No."

"How was Miami?" I asked. "Nice outfit, by the way."

"This?" She made a face. "It's a nothing of a dress. And Miami is the same—hot, big, crowded. I could die happy never visiting again."

She looked at the professor, who seemed mesmerized by his view of the gray beach. "Professor," she said, her tone more pointed. "A woman could grow old and die waiting for you to notice her."

Something in her tone must have registered with him because he turned his head and blinked. "I'm so sorry. Were you speaking to me?"

She laughed, once again the pleasant hostess. "Jacob and I are so pleased to have you in our home. We have wanted to talk to you about our Andi."

Alarm filled the professor's eyes. He shifted his gaze to me, so I stepped behind Safta and mouthed *Just humor her, will you?*

"You know," Safta said, oblivious to the professor's discomfort, "we are people of the Book, so we love learning. Do you know what is a Jewish dropout? A boy who didn't get his Ph.D. But the girls—ah, the girls. Surely you know some nice Jewish boy who needs a beautiful wife like my granddaughter the genius?"

The professor's brows rushed together. "Andi wants a husband?"

"Not yet, I don't." I wrapped my fingers around my grandmother's soft upper arm. "Safta, I think I'm going to take the professor for a walk. He ought to see the beach while he's here."

Safta blinked. "Like they don't have a beach in California?"

"Not like ours, they don't." I took the can of almonds from the professor, set it on the kitchen island, and jerked my head toward the door. "Let's go, professor. Everyone needs to see the Gulf at least once."

"When you come back, we talk," Safta said, waving us away.

The professor hesitated only a moment, then darted toward the door. Apparently he'd realized that a walk in drizzling rain was vastly preferable to remaining in the house with my plain-spoken grandmother.

Chapter 2

The rain had let up by the time the professor and I crossed the pool deck, but the professor insisted that we grab an umbrella from the old milk can by the door. "I'm not a tourist," he insisted. "I don't need to experience rain and sand to appreciate their existence."

Though he would have denied it, I had a feeling he grabbed the umbrella because he didn't want me to get wet. Though he was technically my employer, at times he treated me more like a daughter—making sure I got enough sleep, reminding me to eat fruits and vegetables, even offering to run background checks on the guys I dated—when I had time to date, that is. Several of my friends had lifted a brow when I told them I'd be traveling around the country with a man old enough to be my father, but within ten minutes of meeting him, they understood that our relationship was in no way romantic. He was my employer, I was his gofer/researcher. And sometimes, especially lately, a surrogate daughter.

By the time we walked past the wide beds of sea oats that separated my grandparents' property from the public beach, we could see a crowd near the water's edge. I was surprised to find so many people out in such bad weather—rain usually sent tourists to the shopping malls. Yet as far as I could see, clumps of people stood at the water's edge and stared at the sand.

The professor squinted toward the crowd. "Did someone drown?"

"Not likely. We'd see lifeguards and boats if they were searching."

When we drew nearer the water, we understood. The waterline was outlined with the narrow bodies of hundreds and hundreds of fish. Their silver bodies tumbled in the wavewash and carpeted the heaving surface of the gulf. The misty air felt heavy, permeated with foreboding.

When we stopped, I studied the fish at my feet and was horrified to note that something—disease or parasite—had removed the fish's eyes. Only round black holes remained.

I covered my mouth as déjà vu sent a shudder up the ladder of my spine. No eyes. Just like Abby in my dream.

I turned away, not wanting the professor to see the

tumultuous emotions that had to be flickering across my face. I was not the sort of person who had prophetic dreams, but this could not be coincidence.

Anxiety swelled like a balloon in my chest, making it hard to breathe.

"Andi?" The professor touched my arm, then looked at my face. "What's wrong?"

How could I explain my premonition to a man who didn't believe in them?

"Um, I used to play on this beach as a child," I said, insignificant words tumbling from my lips. "And I've never seen anything like this. Occasionally my grandparents would point out an empty turtle shell or a bird that had become entangled in fishing line, but the beach always brimmed with more life than death. I saw jellyfish and stingrays and even an occasional tiger shark, but this—this is a monumental disaster."

I finally met the professor's gaze, hoping he might have a logical explanation, but in his eyes I saw a confusion that matched my own.

I walked a few yards down the beach and approached another group of onlookers. They were talking about pollution and red tide; one man insisted this disaster was the result of global warming. I was about to ask if he had documentation to back up his assertion when from the corner of my eye I spotted a man and woman approaching. The woman wore a blazer and skirt—definitely not beach apparel—and the man carried a video camera on his shoulder.

"This good?" The woman stopped in a deserted area and turned her back to the water. The cameraman retreated a few feet, then held up four fingers and began counting down. *Three, two—*

"Michelle Tybee here, reporting for Channel 13

news," the woman said, pulling back her wind-blown hair. "Residents of Indian Rocks Beach are out on the sand today, stunned and sorrowful to see evidence of a mass die-off on their pristine shores. As of yet there are no answers for this mysterious occurrence, but these Florida residents are dismayed to find themselves among the growing number of people who have stepped outside their homes and discovered hundreds, if not thousands, of dead animals on the streets and lawns of their neighborhoods. Are we witnessing the evidence of global warming? Are we unknowingly causing the deaths of the animals who share our planet? Is the government conducting secret experiments and wreaking devastation within our own borders? No one knows the answer, but the world waits for an explanation. As do these concerned beachgoers."

The camera man nodded and the reporter flung back her hair again, then bent to take off her shoe and shake out the sand. In search of an answer, I hurried forward. "Hello? May I ask you something?"

She gave me a polite smile. "I'm sorry, but we've finished our interviews for this piece."

"Um, no, I don't want to be on camera. I just wondered if anyone official has been out to investigate. Surely someone has done a necropsy on these fish to determine the cause of death—"

"I wouldn't know." The reporter shrugged. "But when someone comes up with an answer, I'm sure we'll report it. Check the news in a couple of days."

I was about to ask if she knew the names of any biological scientists in the area, but was distracted by something that fell at my feet. I stepped back and saw a red-winged blackbird dead on the ground. Like the fish, it had no eyes. I blinked, unable to believe I'd just missed being hit by the bird, then I heard another soft plop a few feet away. Another dead bird. Then another hit the arm of the reporter. She shrieked, lifted her hands over her head, and gazed at the sky. "What the—"

Like dark, oversized rain drops, a shower of dead birds fell onto the water and sand, sending us humans scrambling for cover.

The professor had come up with an explanation by the time we reached the beach house. "The weather." He pointed upward. "A storm front moved in, swept up a flock of birds, and exposed them to freezing temperatures or a sudden variation in barometric pressure. I'm no zoologist or meteorologist, but I'm sure the explanation has something to do with this bit of bad weather."

"Really? Then why doesn't every thunderstorm result in dead animals?" I stopped to open the sliding door, then faced him. "And what happened to their eyes?"

He blew out his breath in weary exasperation, then dropped the umbrella back into the milk can. "Ask someone who cares."

I watched as he walked through the kitchen and turned toward the hallway that led to his guest room. He wanted to be alone; maybe he would sleep. Maybe the weirdness on the beach had brought back too many troubling memories.

I, however, would not surrender to despondency. I found a note from Safta on the counter—she and Sabba had run to the grocery—I went into the living room and turned on the TV, switched to the local news, and opened my laptop. I did a Google search for "mass animal deaths," and within a couple of nanoseconds I found several pages listing dozens of mass die-offs—of crabs, birds, fish, dolphin, starfish, whales, even cattle, elk, and sheep. I read about cows who'd been struck by lightning while standing under a tree, and sheep who had blindly followed-the-leader off a cliff and plunged to their deaths.

Then I read that mass animal deaths, even so-called animal suicides, had begun to increase at an alarming rate. I found a map labeled with the locations of mass deaths and saw that they were occurring all over the world, but the majority were being reported in "modern" countries. Scientists offered various explanations, of course—polluted water, algae blooms, submarine sonar experiments, global warning/climate change, or perhaps a combination of all those elements.

Staring at the global map with its heavy spattering of dots, I felt an odd tightening at the base of my skull. For some reason—or maybe a host of reasons—Earth's animals were perishing, and it seemed logical to assume humans would be affected next. Like the canaries coal miners kept below ground to signal a dangerous rise in toxic gases, certain species were dying because something was wrong with our environment. But what? And why had animals begun to die all over the planet?

I moused over the United States, then zoomed in to separate the dots that blanketed the map. The dots separated, so I enlarged the selection until the map of the United States filled my laptop screen.

Then I saw it: the gentle curve and swirl of the golden ratio. *Phi,* the formula said to govern the cosmos. The arrangement found everywhere in nature and purported to be the very definition of beauty.

I leaned back and closed my eyes, struggling to understand what I was seeing. How could these be natural events if caused by climate change? Was I seeing proof of chaos theory, or was a higher law at work? In either case, if the pattern continued, it would keep spiraling until every place was affected, until every animal species suffered. Each creature had its place in the food chain, and you couldn't eradicate one without affecting the entire ecosystem . . .

My thoughts shifted as the professor entered the living room and dropped into Sabba's favorite chair. "Something I ate," he said, pounding his chest with his fist, "didn't agree with me. I just had the strangest nightmare, and I rarely dream in my power naps."

My pulse quickened. "What'd you see?"

"That kid—remember? Sridhar, the lucid dreamer from the Institute. He was calling to me, trying to say something. I couldn't understand him, but I had the distinct feeling that he was trying to warn me about something."

"That doesn't sound very nightmarish."

"You didn't see what I saw." He shuddered. "The kid had no eyes."

The professor went on, trying to imitate whatever sounds the dream Sridhar had been making, but my thoughts turned to Brenda and Tank. When we'd met Sridhar, he'd explained that the Institute had trained him to influence other people's dreams . . . was he trying to send a message to the professor? Was he also sending messages to me?

I lowered my hand and found Abby's head—she was on the floor at my side. She used to stretch out by my desk chair and take long naps, but now she lay with her head erect, her ears pointed forward, her eyes watchful.

I scratched her forehead, expecting her to close her eyes and groan in gratitude, but after only a second or two, she leapt to her feet, walked through the kitchen, and sat at the sliding glass doors, her attention fixed on something outside.

Even the professor noticed. "I thought Labs were mellow, but your dog seems unusually high-strung."

"She's not, usually." I got up and went to see what Abby was watching. Looking through the wide panes of glass, I saw nothing unusual—the sea oats, swaying in the breeze, the gentle surf, a bearded guy with a metal detector walking over the sand.

A low growl rumbled in Abby's throat.

"It's just a metal detector," I told her. "We see those all the time."

She continued to growl. When the bearded guy moved out of our view, I expected Abby to relax, but she stood, hair rising at the back of her neck. She barked in the deep, hoarse tone she used as a warning, but though I kept my eyes on the beach, I saw nothing that should have alarmed her.

But her apprehension was contagious. The dreams . . . Sridhar . . . the dead animals. Something was out of kilter in the universe, and, judging by Abby's reaction, the danger loomed right outside our door. The professor and I seemed to be in the middle of a verifiable mystery, and if we were, we needed the others.

"Professor?" I called over my shoulder. "Could you understand *anything* Sridhar was trying to tell you?"

I heard the soft sound of his loafers on the tiled floor behind me. "If I had to guess," he said, "he might have been saying 'prepare the eight.'"

I turned. "The *eight*? Eight what?"

He shrugged. "I have never been one to place much stock in dreams, let alone dream languages."

"Eight." I ran through the multiples. "Sixteen, twenty-four, thirty-two, forty, forty-eight—"

"Then again," the professor interrupted, "he might have said 'beware the rate.'"

I blinked.

"Or 'look there your fate.' Or 'aware the bait'."

I groaned. He was toying with me now, making fun of my affinity for numbers and patterns.

"Thanks for your help," I told him, my tone frosty. "I'll take it from here."

He chuckled and went back to the living room, where he'd probably pick up his book or take another nap. And while he tried to take his mind off the bizarre occurrences that we'd encountered, I would think about Brenda, Tank, and Daniel . . .

We had left Port Avalon feeling that we might not ever see each other again, but now I was beginning to believe we were meant to be together. But how was that possible? Brenda lived in California, and Tank—I couldn't remember exactly where he was living, but I knew he was playing football in the Northwest. Daniel was a resident at the Norquist Center for Behavioral Health, how was it even possible for us to come together again?

The impossible, Sabba always said, began with a single step toward the possible.

I bit my lower lip, then made a decision. Sabba had a jet, and he'd do anything for me. Even if it meant going to the end of the earth to fetch my friends.

Chapter 3

"Brenda?" I tried to keep my voice light, not wanting to frighten her with my theory of looming disaster. "Hey, it's Andi. Listen, something's come up, and I think the group needs to get together right away. I'm in Florida at my grandparents' beach house, and my grandfather is willing to send his plane for you—"

"I'd love to help you out—" I heard the crack of her gum—"but I have a tat scheduled for tomorrow. It's a five-hour-gig, maybe more. I gotta pay the bills, you know?"

My heart sank. Until that instant, I hadn't realized how much I was counting on her. "Well—"

"Hang on a sec."

I waited, barely daring to breathe, and after a minute Brenda spoke again. "You're not gonna believe this," she said, a wry note in her voice, "but my client just texted me. He's canceling because his girlfriend threw a fit about the tat, but he's going to pay me anyway." She snorted. "So yeah, I guess I'm good to go wherever. Did you mention a private plane?"

"Yes." I sighed in relief. "I'll call Tank, too. And I have a feeling we need Daniel with us. I have *no* idea how to make that happen—"

"Leave it to me," Brenda said. "I took Daniel back to the hospital after our last little reunion, so those people know me. I'll pick him up."

I wasn't sure how she would get Daniel out of the hospital, but I had a feeling Brenda could manage almost anything.

"Okay. I'll give my grandfather your number so he make the arrangements."

After hanging up with her, I dialed Tank's phone and was surprised when he answered right away. "'Lo?"

"Tank, it's Andi. I know you're probably in the middle of football and everything, but—"

"I'm not," Tank said. "Broke my toe last week. I'm benched."

"Wow." I paused to catch my breath. "Sorry about that."

"'Sokay. I'm third string, so it's not like the team's depending on me. Coach says I can use the rest of the season to lift weights and work out. And, you know, go to school."

"Can you walk?"

He laughed. "Sure. Just not very fast. And not very, you know, smoothly."

"Well . . ." I hesitated. "I hate to ask, with you being wounded and all, but I think the group needs to get together. Can you join us tomorrow?"

"Man, I hate to say this, but I promised the lady downstairs that I'd take her to the doctor tomorrow. She's old, so she doesn't drive. When I found out she couldn't get to the doctor, well—" he chuckled. "You know."

"Yeah." I tried to keep my disappointment out of my voice. "Brenda's coming, and she's bringing Daniel. And the professor's already here. So all we need is you."

"Sorry about that. I really am."

I waited, unable to accept that Tank wouldn't be joining us. The idea was inconceivable, like imagining yin without yang, warp without weft . . .

I heard noise in the background—an increasingly shrill siren. "Where are you, Tank? Sounds like you're in the middle of a traffic accident."

"Maybe. I'm almost home, but there's an ambulance at my building. Hang on a minute."

I waited, staring at the ceiling, and heard muffled voices, sounds of movement, and the heavy thunk of something like a car door. Then I heard the siren again, even louder this time.

"Andi?"

I blew out a breath. "I thought maybe you'd broken something else."

"No, no—that was my neighbor. She slipped in her kitchen and fell, but someone heard her shouting and called 911. She's on her way to the hospital now."

Despite the worry in Tank's voice, my spirits

began to rise. "So . . . you don't have to take her to the doctor tomorrow, do you?"

Tank hesitated, then laughed. "I guess I don't."

"So you can join us."

He hesitated again, then cleared his throat. "Gosh, Andi, I hate to be a bad sport, but I can't afford a plane ticket to Florida. I just—"

"My grandfather is sending his jet to get Brenda and Daniel, and they'll get you, too. Just let us know the nearest airport, and we'll have the pilot pick you up."

"Wow." Tank's pleased surprise rolled over the line. "Well shucks, how can I say no? I'll be there. Let me figure out where the closest airport is, then I'll call you back."

"Great. I'll see you tomorrow night."

I clicked off the call, even more convinced that the five of us were meant to be together—and together *here*.

Chapter 4

That night at dinner, Safta and Sabba listened in shocked silence as I described the dead, eyeless animals on the beach, then Safta shook her head. "Such a death shouldn't happen to a tadpole," she said. "All those birds and fishes. What could have done such a thing?"

"Do you really want to know?" The professor rested his fingers on the table and drummed them as he looked from Safta to Sabba.

Sabba lifted a bushy brow. "And you have the answer?"

The professor nodded. "It's no surprise—people

have been talking about the situation for years now. Climate change is undoubtedly responsible for all the things we are seeing—the strange weather patterns, the animal deaths, the earthquakes. Mankind's damage to our planet has reached a critical stage, and the sentinel species are being affected. Very simple."

I dropped my fork and stared at him. I'd been working for the professor for nearly a year, and I liked him despite his tendency to be stubborn. The man was brilliant, unswervingly logical, and fluent in mathematics, physics, and chemistry, but for the first time in months, I didn't agree with him.

"Professor—" I folded my hands—"this afternoon I studied a map of places where mass animal deaths have occurred. I found another map of nations who have contributed the most to climate change. I might find your theory more believable if the patterns matched, but they're not even close. The animal deaths have occurred almost everywhere and there is no observable connection."

The professor looked at me a moment, thought narrowing his eyes, then he shook his head. "It's apples and oranges, Andi. Climate change isn't evidenced as strongly in the most polluting nations because it's in the more agrarian nations where the effects of climate change will be felt. In places where people farm for a living, a lack of rainfall spells disaster. And droughts happen because of climate change."

I didn't want to argue with him in front of my grandparents, but my gut told me I was right. I closed my eyes and saw both maps on the back of my eyelids—the map displaying countries with the most carbon dioxide emissions highlighted the United

States, Russia, Australia, and Saudi Arabia. An accompanying map displaying countries most affected by climate change marked Saudi Arabia along with parts of Africa, South America, and the U.S. Neither map displayed any pattern resembling the golden ratio.

The map of mass animal deaths did not correlate with the maps of climate change. The United States and England had experienced dozens of animal die-offs, along with areas of Australia, South America, and the Arabian peninsula. But the Near East—Thailand, Japan, North and South Korea—had experienced several mass animal deaths, and those countries weren't featured on either of the climate change maps.

"Man not only has the power to change human life," the professor was telling my grandparents, "but for the first time in history we now have the power to change our planet. Unfortunately, most of our changes have been destructive because we haven't realized the significance of our actions. In the future, however, mankind will make great strides to preserve the earth and improve our standard of living."

"I blame it all on the Republicans." Sabba's face flushed as he leaned across the table. "For years they have refused to believe climate change was taking place."

"And should the Democrats get off scot-free?" Safta waved her fork at Sabba. "For years Al Gore has declared that the North Pole was going to melt—and I just read that it's getting bigger. The North Pole, melt?" She harrumphed. "Al Gore should live so long."

I slid lower in my chair and stirred my mashed

potatoes, still hot from the KFC bag. Now that the conversation had turned political, my grandparents would argue with each other for another hour, forgetting all about me and our guest.

I glanced at the professor and saw that he was busy cutting up his fried chicken. He wasn't political, as far as I knew, but he could be as immoveable as Sabba and Safta. If he had his way, logic would rule the universe and chaos would be obliterated.

Of course, lately the professor had learned that logic didn't always win the day.

Over by the sliding door that opened to the deck, Abby was still sitting and staring out the window. Occasionally she pawed at the glass, then went back to watching. I tried calling her to my side, but each time I said her name, she looked at me, whined as if begging me to understand, and went back to her vigil.

Every whine pebbled my skin with gooseflesh.

My heart twisted as memory carried me back to all the days I used to sit with her on the deck before I left for college. She'd been my best friend in those days. When no one in high school cared to befriend the geeky girl with explosive red-hair, Abby had been my constant companion and very best friend. She had guarded my secrets and listened to my dreams. She had warmed my feet while I studied and licked up the cookie crumbs from my bedroom carpet. My heart ached for her when I went away to school, but she was always waiting when I came home. We picked up where we'd left off, and for years I half-believed that time stopped for Abby while I was away.

Yesterday, however, Abby had given me an enthusiastic greeting, then gone straight to the sliding glass door to stare out at the beach.

Just like she was doing now. Just like she'd done in my dream.

I sank even lower in my chair and studied her, wondering what she knew that I didn't.

Chapter 5

Picking up dead birds wasn't my idea of a good time, but I figured someone had to do it. Sabba had kept his promise and sent his private plane to pick up Brenda, Daniel, and Tank. Until they arrived, I had nothing to do but play Mah-Jongg with Safta and her friends, watch the professor read, or venture out to the beach.

So I got up early, pulled a pair of shorts and a tee shirt from my old dresser, and slipped into a battered pair of sneakers I found in the closet. I smeared sunblock on my nose (redheads tend to burn easily, even in October) and pulled one of Safta's battered straw hats from a hook in the laundry room. I grabbed a couple of trash bags from a cabinet, then strode out across the deck and went down to the beach.

I wasn't alone. The beach was spotted with curious onlookers and social do-gooders. I smiled a "me, too" smile at a girl dressed a lot like I was, then took a pair of rubber gloves from a table and read the sheet of instructions someone had posted:

1. Don't touch dead birds or fish with bare hands.
No kidding.
2. Don't throw dead birds or fish back into the water.
Wouldn't that defeat the purpose?
3. Place all dead birds and fish in a trash bag, then close securely. Leave bags by the life guard stand; someone from the Pinellas Fish and Game Department will pick them up later.

Simple enough. I powered on my iPhone, put the earbuds in my ears, then slipped my hands into the flimsy gloves and set out for a section of beach still littered with dead animals. The music carried my thoughts away as I knelt to clear the area around me. The fish's empty eye sockets seemed to accuse me—of what? If I'd known what killed them, I would have done something to help. Anyone would. Anyone who loved animals, that is.

After a while I stopped picking up fish one by one and began to gather them by handfuls. How many yards, I wondered, did this carpet of dead fish extend? And the birds—the tide had pushed most of them farther up the beach, but their little bodies littered the dunes several yards beyond the water's edge. If disease or climate conditions had caused their deaths, why had they only fallen here? Why hadn't they landed in my grandparents' front yard, or on the roadways? What had caused them to fall in this particular spot?

And most important, what had happened to their eyes?

The odor of decaying flesh was strong enough to overpower the tang of sea air, but after a while I grew numb to it. Numb enough that I was able to pick up a single bird, hold it in my gloved left palm, and bring it close to my face, using my right hand to probe its feathery little body. Like the fish, the bird had holes where his eyes should have been. In addition, this bird's little beak appeared cracked and some sort of brown liquid dribbled from its nostrils. The little body felt like a feathery bag of air in my hand.

When I heard the unexpected sound of a vehicle on the beach, I turned and looked behind me. A white van had pulled up near the lifeguard stand, and two men in hazmat uniforms had stepped onto the beach. Hazmats? Did these guys know something we didn't?

I dropped the little bird's body into my bag and went over to check out the new arrivals.

The van had no markings or identification on it, so for a while I simply watched the men dressed in white from head to toe. They walked over the sand as I had, but they used a long-handled tool to pick up the dead animals, then they put certain specimens into individual bags. After sealing each bag, they wrote something on it—probably date and time—and placed the sealed specimens in a cooler.

I gave them space to pick up a few corpses, then pulled out my earbuds and walked up to the closest guy. "Hi," I said, smiling. "Who are you and where are you from?"

He blinked at me as if I were a Martian who'd suddenly come up and introduced myself. For a moment he seemed taken aback, then he fumbled with his hazmat helmet and pulled it off. "Steve Laughlin," he said, his cheeks brightening as if he had suddenly realized how silly he looked in all that protective gear. "We're from the University of Tampa."

"Oh." I laughed. "I thought you were from the government."

He laughed, too. "Not by a long shot. The government's probably been here and gone already, leaving us to clean up the mess. This thing has made our biology department curious, and since it happened in our own backyard—"

"I get it. I'm curious, too." I felt the corner of my mouth rise in a half-smile. Steve Laughlin looked like a professional geek—my kind of guy. "Don't you feel a little overdressed? I mean, no one has even hinted that these animals died from contagion."

"No one has said they *didn't*." Steve smiled back at me, apparently recognizing a kindred spirit. "I've always found it better to err on the side of caution."

I nodded. "Listen, Steve—you got a pen?"

He pulled one from his pocket, and I took it. "I'm visiting the area with my boss, Professor James McKinney. We're keen to know more about this event, and if you learn anything, we'd appreciate it if you'd give us a call." I grabbed his gloved hand and pulled it toward me, then wrote on the back of his white glove. "This is my cell number? Will you call me?"

His eyes glinted with interest—more than a purely scientific interest, it seemed to me. "I'll call if you'll tell me your name."

"Andi." I released his hand and held out his pen. "Don't forget—I have friends who will be truly intrigued by whatever you learn."

His mouth curved in a slow smile. "Andi. Got a last name to go with that?"

"Maybe." I picked up my trash bag and waved. "Maybe you'll find out when you call."

Chapter 6

I'd gone maybe a mile down the beach when I turned
to check the time. The sun stood about midway down
the horizon, so Safta would nearly be finished
packing.

Once my grandparents learned that I needed to
invite several people to the house, they had graciously
offered to leave us and spend a couple of days at their
Manhattan apartment. Since Sabba had retired, Safta
said, he didn't get to New York as often as he wanted
to.

"I hate to put you out," I told them. "After all, I
came here to see you."

"Listen, *bubeleh*," Safta said, "us you can see any time. I see the shadows on your face, and I think your friends can help you now. Me, I will never understand the things you talk about, so you stay while we go. We will come back in a couple of days."

I reluctantly agreed to accept their offer.

Since my grandparents were leaving us alone in the house, I planned to put Tank in my grandparents' room, give the two guest rooms to the professor and Brenda, and bunk Daniel in Sabba's den, which was close to where Brenda would be sleeping. I would remain in my old room, which still looked pretty much as it did when I left for college.

Now I squinted at people on the beach. Dozens of strangers were walking along the water's edge, but I spotted four familiar shapes coming from the house—little Daniel, Brenda, the professor, and Tank, who hobbled over the sand like a giant with a broken toe . . . because that's what he was.

I lifted Safta's sunhat and waved it, then clapped it back on my head and strode toward them. I felt as giddy as a kid and I couldn't say why, but seeing the others made me feel a lot less melancholy.

I dropped my trash bag in the sand and ran to hug them—Brenda first, then Tank, and then Daniel. I grinned at the professor, who gave me a grudging smile as if he, too, were glad to be a part of this inexplicable team.

"Eew!" Brenda backed away, shaking her head. "I hate to say this, but you stink."

Tank was too much of a gentleman to say anything about the smell, but the strangled look on his face told me he was trying hard not to inhale.

"Andrea," the professor said, "I don't know how

you can stand it out here. Come back to the house, take a shower, and let's talk. Your grandmother has ordered dinner, which should be arriving shortly."

"You bet." I grinned around the circle of friendly faces. "Just let me dump my collection bag at the lifeguard stand."

An hour later I was clean, perfumed, and sitting at the head of Safta's dinner table. She had ordered several Chinese dishes, which waited on a lazy Susan along with a selection of chopsticks and a note staying "Welcome to the Beach House."

"In a place this fancy, I know we're supposed to use good manners," Brenda said, glancing around, "so I'll be good and not smoke in the house. But I'm starving, so if you'll pass your plates, I'll slap on some rice. Daniel, you want brown rice or white?"

Daniel shifted his gaze from the sliding glass door to look at her, but didn't respond.

Brenda nodded. "Okay, white rice it is. Cowboy, what do you want, a bowlful of everything?"

While Brenda served, I leaned back and studied her and Daniel. Something had happened between them since we were last together—the tenuous bond they established in Port Avalon was far stronger now. I could see it in the way her body curved toward him and in the way his eyes followed her as she served everyone else. Maybe he'd been afraid to fly this morning and she comforted him. Maybe he'd begun to see her as a surrogate mother. One thing I knew for sure—if the kid had managed to get inside her heart, he was the only one of us who had.

And Daniel—in Port Avalon, he had been accompanied by an invisible friend . . . a rather large friend who didn't care for the name *Harvey*. If Daniel's imperceptible protector had come along on this trip, apparently he hadn't joined us for dinner.

Brenda was watching Tank inhale a plate of Kung Pao chicken when I caught her attention. "By the way, how'd you get Daniel out of the hospital?"

She smirked. "You wouldn't believe it."

"Give us a try."

Brenda glanced around the table, then snorted. "Okay. So last time when I took Daniel back to the hospital, I had to explain why he was with me, right? So I told them that I was his aunt, and I was steamin' mad that they'd let that other couple sign him out without providing any kind of identification. I showed them a newspaper article about the murders in Port Avalon, and I told 'em Daniel had been in the middle of all that. Well." She smiled. "They were so terrified by my threats of a lawsuit that they never asked to see anything from me. I had them put me down as Daniel's aunt, and I told them that if they ever released him to anybody but me, I'd sue the lab coats right off their pimply backsides. You should have seen 'em scampering to take care of the boy after that."

"That hardly seems logical." The professor smiled, but his eyes softened when he looked at the boy. "Surely his parents are listed in his file. I'm sure there are certain custody orders, medical releases—"

"That's the thing, Doc." Brenda leaned toward us and lowered her voice to a rough whisper. "That hospital is like the end of the earth. One look around and you know that nobody is comin' for any of those patients. I get the feelin' that Norquist is the kind of place where they put people nobody ever wants to see again."

A low rumble came from deep in the professor's throat.

"So this time when I went to get him," Brenda went on, "I sashayed right up to the desk and said I was Daniel's aunt and I'd come to take him out for a few days. The girl looked at me like I had a hole in the head, but then she called over some Deputy Dog security guard. I recognized him—he'd been on duty the last time—and he said, 'Oh, yeah, she's his aunt. She's cool.' And then the girl says, 'But I don't have her on his approved visitor list,' and the guard says, 'Then you'd better *get* her on his approved list.' So the next thing I know, I'm on some kind of list, and they're bringing Daniel out to me. The girl is watching me, though, probably thinking that Daniel will freak out or something if he doesn't know me, but he comes right over, slides his hand into mine, and off we go, just like Bonnie and Clyde."

The professor cleared his throat. "I'd choose another metaphorical paring, if I were you. Bonnie and Clyde didn't end well."

Brenda's eyes sparked with annoyance. She picked up her fork, and for an instant I worried that she might lean across the table and stab the professor with it.

"Pinocchio and Jimmy Cricket?" Tank smiled, easing the tension. "They had a happy ending."

"Indeed." The professor nodded. "And the metaphor is more apt, considering the cricket served as the puppet's conscience. In a way, you are serving as the boy's window to the world."

Brenda lowered her fork and shot me a *is he for real?* look, and I shrugged. Being a professor, my boss often felt inclined to correct others, and Brenda didn't like being corrected.

Few people did.

"So, Miss Andi." Tank stopped shoveling food long enough to look over at me. "Why are we here?"

I bit my lip, hoping I could explain what I felt in my gut. "It all started when I had a horrible dream about Abby losing her eyes. Scarcely an hour later the dead fish washed up and something had destroyed all their eyes. That was bizarre enough, but within minutes, dead birds started falling out of the sky, also without eyes. Then I got a strong feeling that the two events were connected—and when the professor said he'd had a dream about Sridhar and *he* had no eyes, I knew I needed you all to help me. I know there's a connection, but I can't figure out what it is."

"So what are we supposed to do?" Brenda asked.

"I have no idea." I raked my hand through my hair and propped my elbow on the table. "But I did some preliminary research and discovered that mass animal deaths are occurring all over the planet, and not only with birds and fish. Cattle, sheep, elk, crabs, oysters, honeybees, seals, starfish, puffins—"

"What's a puffin?" Tank asked.

"A kind of sea bird," I answered. "Cute little things."

Tank shifted in his seat. "Those other animals— did they lose their eyeballs, too?"

I shook my head. "I don't think so. They were just . . . dead."

"Yes, animals are dying." The professor folded his hands. "But mass animal deaths have occurred throughout the centuries. Look at what happened to the dinosaurs."

I blinked. I hadn't considered the dinosaurs, though I knew the cause for their extinction was hotly debated. Some scientists believed they died before the emergence of human beings when a meteor hit the earth; others believed the dinosaurs perished in an ancient flood. I didn't want to get into a debate about dinosaurs over dinner—the professor would certainly prevail, and we'd be distracted from the work we were supposed to be doing.

"Yes, the dinosaurs died," I admitted, "but now all kinds of animals are dying."

"Like the buffalo?" Tank asked.

I gave him a patient smile. "There's no mystery about why the buffalo nearly died out," I reminded him. "People killed them, and when they stopped, the buffalo herds came back. It's the same reason elephants and gorillas are dying now. But we don't understand why these other deaths are occurring."

"I'm sure there's a good reason," Brenda said, though she sounded anything *but* sure. "I'm no scientist, but don't they blame these things on pollution, red tides, stuff like that?"

"Sometimes they can find a reason for one situation," I pointed out, "but so many? And there's— something else."

I pressed my lips together, wondering if they'd laugh.

Brenda made an impatient gesture. "What?"

"A pattern," I said. "The golden mean. I was looking at map of animal deaths, and there were dozens of dots all over the map. So I zoomed in and naturally the dots spread out. That's when I saw the curved spiral that looks like the inside of a sea shell— the golden mean. It occurs all over the place in nature, and it's nature's way of performing her work efficiently. Which means that if nature is killing the animals, she will efficiently meet her goals and we humans might be next."

"Whoa." Brenda held up both hands. "Step it back. I'm not getting this."

"Let me help." The professor leaned back in his chair and gave me a wry smile. "You know how Andi loves her patterns. But while the brain *does* tend to seek patterns in everything from clouds to breakfast toast, apophenia is not a true gift. We yearn for patterns because humans yearn for predictability."

"It *is* a real gift," I insisted. "I don't see the face of Jesus in mushrooms, I see . . . structures and schemes. And with all due respect, professor, just because scientists debunk the idea of apophenia doesn't make it any less real."

Brenda and Tank shifted their gazes from me to the professor and then back to me, probably debating which one of us they should believe. Daniel just kept eating.

Brenda looked at Tank. "Maybe it doesn't matter," she said. "What matters is that next bit she mentioned—if she's right about all the animals dying and we're next, well, that's freakin' *interesting*."

Tank snorted. "Yeah. So—what *is* this mean thing?"

"The golden mean," I explained, "sometimes called the golden ratio. Philosophers consider it a definition of beauty; mathematicians call it *phi*. Fibonacci explained it as a series in which every number is the sum of the two numbers preceding it, like this: 1, 1, 2, 3, 5, 8, 13, 21, 34, 55 and so on. This series seems to be sort of a key for organisms in nature. For instance, consider flowers: the lily has three petals, buttercups have five, the chicory has twenty-one, the daisy has thirty-four, and so on. And seed heads, like sunflowers? In order to pack the seeds in so that no space is wasted and every seed receives an adequate amount of sunlight, nature needed to determine the perfect mathematical ratio for placing and positioning seeds. That ratio is 0.618034—the ratio of phi, the golden mean. That ratio results in the spiral you see in pinecones, sunflower seeds, sea shells, even hurricanes. Artists and photographers use it in composition; architects plan buildings around it. It's perfection; completion. It's the way nature gets things done."

"It's genius." Tank grinned. "And only a master creator could have figured that stuff out."

Brenda stared at me, a hard line between her brows. Clearly, she thought I was nuts.

"Let me show you." I stood and grabbed my laptop from the kitchen counter, then pulled up an illustration of the golden mean.

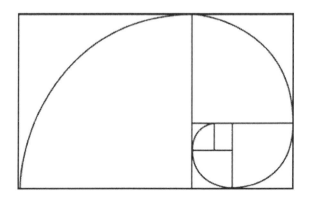

"Okay." Brenda nodded. "I may not understand all

this, but it's enough that you do. But what makes you think these animal deaths have anything to do with pinecones and hurricanes?"

"Because of the pattern." On my laptop, I opened the map of animal deaths. Zooming in as before, I focused on a cluster in the south, then ran my finger over it, connecting the dots in the arch and resultant swirl.

I think even Tank was impressed.

Brenda tilted her head. "Cool."

"Is it? The golden mean is Nature in no-nonsense mode. What if she is killing the animals?"

"I wish you'd stop talking about Nature like it's a person," Tank mumbled. "Nature isn't a person, it's a creation. If someone is doin' something, it has to be the creator."

"What if the operative force is mankind?" the professor said. "What if people have unknowingly triggered something that might result in the loss of all life on the planet?"

After a moment of heavy silence, Brenda laughed, Tank looked baffled, and the professor smirked. Even Daniel, who usually wore a blank look, seemed to have a small smile on his face. I guess that's what happens when ants look up at the rain and talk about how they might make it stop.

"We're not scientists," Brenda said, still snickering. "If what you're saying is true, what are idiots like us supposed to do about it?"

The professor stiffened. "I beg your pardon. *You* may not aspire to be an example of intelligent human life, but others—"

"Here we go," Brenda said, looking at me. "Just when I thought we were beginning to get along."

"Are we gonna be travelin' everywhere, checking out dead animals?" Tank asked.

I held up my hands, unable to handle all of them at once. "I don't know what we do next. I only know I was supposed to invite you here because Sridhar might be trying to reach us. Can we just leave it at that for now? Do you think we can spend a couple of days here without insulting each other?"

The others looked around the table, then Brenda's mouth curved in a smile. "I always did want a Florida vacation. Spending a couple of days in this big ol' beach house is all right by me."

The professor crossed his arms and lowered his chin, his way of capitulating. He was willing to humor me.

Only Tank seemed to think I might be onto something. He looked at me, his eyes shining with simple faith, then he nodded. "All right, Miss Andi, I'm in. And I'm kinda excited to see what happens tomorrow."

I blew out a breath, hoping I hadn't brought them all down here for nothing. If I was wrong about seeing the golden ratio, or if I had misinterpreted what it meant, they'd never trust me again.

Chapter 7

The next morning, our agenda crystalized the moment Tank picked up a copy of the local newspaper. "Winter the dolphin lives around here?" He grinned at me. "I saw both of those *Dolphin Tale* movies and loved 'em. Can we go see him?"

Brenda looked up, her eyes narrowed. "Who's Winter?"

"That famous dolphin who lost its tail," Tank said. "Now he wears a prosthetic."

The aquarium . . . that gave me an idea. I looked at Daniel, who was finishing up a bowl of Lucky Charms. "Feel like a trip to Clearwater?"

Daniel's eyes lit, and he looked to Brenda. I had a feeling that a local tourist attraction was the last thing on her priority list, but who could resist the look in Daniel's eyes?

"Why not?" Brenda shrugged. "Nuthin' else to do."

I knew the professor wouldn't want to go, but he'd finished the book on chaos theory and would be bored senseless sitting around the house. "All right," he said, sighing heavily. "As long as we stop by a store so I can pick up a raincoat. I don't want to get wet in one of those silly dolphin shows."

"Take one of the umbrellas," I suggested. "And don't sit down front."

The lines at the aquarium were longer than I expected, and the show every bit as wet as the professor feared. I'd been to the aquarium many times as a child, so I spent most of the hour looking around. Tank seemed entranced by the show, frequently grinning and applauding, while the professor appeared to be in danger of nodding off. Daniel watched the dolphin trainers intently while Brenda scribbled in her program.

It wasn't until the show was over and we stood to file out of the bleacher seats that I caught a glimpse of what Brenda had been doing. She'd drawn a face—a young man, probably in his early thirties, with stringy hair, round eyes, and a scorpion tattoo on his neck.

I elbowed her as we slowly inched forward. "That a client of yours?"

She glanced at the drawing, then quickly rolled up her program. "No."

"A friend?"

She shook her head.

"Someone you'd like to meet?"

She turned on me with the fury of a tigress. "It's

nobody, okay? It's just a face. Don't make a big deal about it."

I put up both hands in surrender and made a mental note: *don't ask Brenda about her doodles.*

When we finally threaded our way out of the mob, we walked over to talk to an aquarium staff member. I pulled out my university ID card and suggested that the professor do the same.

"Hi, I'd like to introduce Dr. James McKinney, Ph.D.," I began, "I'm Andi Goldstein, his assistant, and these are our friends. We're researching mass animal deaths and wondered if we could talk to someone on your staff who might be familiar with the animal die-offs at Indian Rocks beach."

The girl who'd narrated the dolphin show glanced at my ID card, then jerked her head toward a nearby door. "Dr. Mathis, our marine biologist, has been following that story. Follow me, and I'll introduce you."

We walked through a doorway labeled "Employees only" and found ourselves in a large room filled with aquariums and several in-ground pools. The aquariums housed turtles and stingrays, and in the pools I saw a small dolphin, a young shark, and a manatee. Several people in shorts and aquarium staff shirts sat on the concrete floor watching the manatee while a diver stood in the pool and stroked the animal.

"What *is* that thing?" Tank's eyes were in danger of falling out of his head. "I've never seen anything like that critter."

"It's a manatee," I told him as we walked over. "They're pretty common in Florida because they're fresh water mammals. According to legend, sailors used to see them and think they were mermaids."

Tank guffawed. "Beggin' your pardon, Miss Andi, but there's no way in the world I'd think that was a mermaid. That animal is—well, it ain't purty."

"Depends on who you ask, Tank."

An older man in a lab coat looked up as we approached, and when the girl introduced the professor, he stood and extended his hand. "Tom Mathis," he said, smiling at us. "Glad to meet you. So how can I help?"

I liked that he didn't add the word *doctor* in front of his name. "The fish and birds at Indian Rocks Beach," I said before the professor could speak and complicate our mission. "Do you have any ideas about what killed them?"

The professor crossed his arms and grinned. "Yes," he said, jerking his head toward me. "What she said."

Mathis took a deep breath and thrust his hands into his pockets. "Wish I did. They brought me a couple of specimens, but I haven't had time to examine them. We're currently facing a crisis with our manatee population—we've lost ten mature adults, several dolphins, and a half-dozen pelicans from a hotspot in the Indian River Lagoon. We don't know what's killing them, either."

"A hotspot?" Brenda crinkled her nose. "Is that anything like a hot spring?"

The marine biologist shook his head. "A hotspot is a dangerous location for wildlife. The entire lagoon used to be heavily polluted, but the river has mostly cleared. Except for that one spot—we still have animals dying in that area, and we're clueless."

"What about their eyes?" Brenda asked. "The

animals from the hotspot—do they still have eyes?"

Mathis drew back. "Why would you ask?"

She lifted a brow. "Because I'm curious?"

The scientist exhaled slowly. "Some of them have their eyes, yes. Others . . . well, we assume they're missing their eyes because decomposition takes place more rapidly in water."

I smiled at Brenda, grateful that she'd asked the question. She'd received a non-answer, but at least we knew that other animals were being affected in the same way as our birds and fish.

"I'm sure you see dead animals all the time," the professor said. "From predators, boat accidents, poisons—"

"Of course we do," Mathis answered. "But not all at once, and not overnight like some of these cases. You might find this interesting."

He gestured to a table covered with plastic bags. Inside each bag I saw a sizable fishing hook. Some of the hooks still had fishing lines attached.

"We pulled all of these from the stomachs of manatees or dolphins," he said, "but the hooks weren't the cause of death. We're still searching for that."

"Global warming?" Tank offered, leaning on a table to take the weight off his injured foot.

Mathis shook his head. "Doubtful. The entire lagoon would be affected by climate conditions." He looked at me and smiled. "I appreciate your interest, but I simply hadn't had a chance to do necropsies on the Indian Rocks animals. I'm sorry I can't be of more help."

"Thank you for your time," I said, pulling one of the professor's cards from my purse. "And if you have a chance to examine those fish or birds, will you give us a call? That card has Dr. McKinney's cell number."

Mathis promised to do what he could and slipped the card in his pocket.

Despite the small confirmations, I led the way out of the building feeling as though I'd led the team on a wild goose chase.

At least Tank and Daniel had enjoyed the dolphin show.

Chapter 8

"So we sat through that dolphin show for nothing," Brenda said, settling into one of my grandparents' deck chairs. She held a sweating glass of lemonade, complete with a paper umbrella, which I'd added as a festive touch. Brenda probably thought I was silly and frivolous, but I was only trying to keep her happy. If we were going to learn anything, we needed to cooperate.

"The trip wasn't a total washout," I insisted.

"Yeah, I got to see Winter the dolphin," Tank said, grinning as he carefully lowered himself into one of the wooden deck chairs. "Man, he's a real inspiration, you know? I know athletes who get hurt and think they're gonna be benched forever, but if a big fish like that can lose his tail and find a way to stay in the game—"

"Your toe's gonna heal, big guy," Brenda interrupted as she fished a pack of cigarettes out of her purse. "Don't worry, you'll play football again."

"And it's a mammal, not a big fish," the professor added. He tilted his head. "By the way, Tank, I seem to recall that you . . . did something to my leg when we first met. It was injured, but you touched it and then it wasn't injured any more."

Tank shrugged as a flush began to creep up from his collar. "Sometimes I can help."

"So why—" the beginning of a smile quirked the professor's mouth—"why haven't you been able to repair your broken toe?"

Tank's flush deepened until the tip of his nose was glowing like Rudolph's. "Um . . . sometimes it doesn't work. So when I couldn't fix it, the team doc taped my toes together and told me to make the best of it."

"You're a good sport." The professor lifted his glass in a mock salute. "Here's to hobbling with dignity."

I looked at Daniel to see if he would smile or say something about the dolphin show, but he sat on the deck steps next to Abby. Both were staring out at the beach, their heads cocked at identical angles.

The sight sent the memory of my dream rushing through me, shivering my skin. But this was reality, and everything was okay. Abby wasn't growling.

"I know," Brenda said, exhaling cigarette smoke as she followed my gaze. "They look cute sitting together like that. I can't figure out if Daniel is copyin' the dog, or if the dog is copyin' Daniel."

I leaned forward to study the pair. When Daniel moved his head to the right, Abby did, too, almost as if they were connected by a string. "I don't know, either," I whispered. "But it is amazing, the way they mirror each other."

"You have to admit, Andi," the professor said, his tone flat and matter-of-fact, "Dr. Mathis was no help today."

"I think he was quite helpful." I straightened. "He gave us another piece of the puzzle, don't you see? He's dealing with bizarre animal die-offs, too, and he even gave us a term for an active location—a hotspot. For some reason, part of the Indian River lagoon is affected when other areas aren't, and maybe that's the same reason this beach is affected when none of the other beaches are."

The professor looked away and sipped his lemonade, a sure sign that he didn't have an answer. When some people met unanswerable logic, they raised their voices. The professor raised a glass. Fortunately, for the last few months his glass had contained only nonalcoholic drinks.

I was about to mention the manatees, but I stopped when Abby growled. The hair at the back of her neck had risen, and she was no longer looking at the beach, but at the sky. Beside her, Daniel stared upward, too, and his hands had curled into fists.

Brenda was saying something about how ugly the manatees were, but I cut her off with a flick of my hand, then pointed to Daniel and Abby. Tank and the professor must have seen my gesture because silence fell over our group as we watched the watchers without any idea of what we were seeing.

In Port Avalon, we had seriously entertained the idea that Daniel's invisible friend was real and the kid could see things the rest of us couldn't. Whether he was seeing into another dimension or a spirit world I couldn't say, but there he was, looking, watching something invisible to my eyes . . .

A chill touched the base of my spine. Was Abby seeing . . . *had* she been seeing . . . the same thing?

"Abby?" I finally said, keeping my voice calm as not to spook her. "Abby, it's okay."

The dog leapt to her feet, her hair bristling along her backbone as she stared up at the cloudless bowl of sky. Daniel stood beside her, his hands knotted so tightly that his arms trembled.

"Abby—"

In an instant, Daniel flinched and ducked and the dog leapt off the porch and soared over the steps. She landed on the sand and took off at a run, barking as though her life depended on being heard. As Abby ran, Daniel moved to the bottom step. For a moment I was afraid he'd take off after the dog, but Brenda took charge: "Daniel—stay with us, baby. It's not safe out there."

I don't know how she knew that, but Daniel trusted her. He stayed on the step.

The professor stood and stared out at the beach. "Do you see anything? Anyone?"

"Not a thing," I whispered, hoping Brenda was wrong about the beach not being safe. But my dream had warned me otherwise.

Tank shook his head. "Just water and waves. A couple of people walked by a few minutes ago, though."

"We're going to be all right," Brenda said, speaking

in the tone a mother might use to soothe a child. I knew she was trying to keep Daniel from running off. We didn't know much about the boy, and though he'd been calm so far, I was pretty sure he could lose control if something flipped his switch. After all, there had to be a reason he was living in a hospital for the mentally ill . . .

I moved to the lowest step so I could grab Daniel if he started to run. From there I saw that Abby had reached the beach, and through the path in the sea oats I could see her running back and forth, barking like crazy at something no one else could see. Then she fell silent and sat on the sand, as if waiting.

"Finally." Relief filled Tank's voice. "When our dog used to bark like crazy, my grandpa always said she was keeping the elephants out of the yard. I'd say, 'But Grandpa, there aren't any elephants,' and he'd grin and say, "Course not. She does a good job, don't she?'"

Is that what Abby had been doing at the window? Keeping something evil away?

I whistled, knowing that the sound would bring her back. She'd come running, tail wagging, because she'd accomplished whatever she'd set out to do. Then I felt a trembling against my leg, and when I looked down, I saw that Daniel had gone pasty white. His arms were thumping at his side, beating against his thighs, and he looked for all the world like he wanted to turn and run back into the house, but loyalty or fear or something held him in place. I was about to take his hand and lead him up the steps, but Abby started barking again so I turned and saw her snarling and flashing her canines, then she ran into the water and started to swim toward the horizon.

The sight was so unexpected and unusual that I forgot about Daniel and stared, watching Abby's bobbing head until it disappeared amid the swells and I couldn't see her anymore.

"Abby!" I screamed her name, my throat tightening. When she didn't answer and I still couldn't see her, I kicked off my shoes. "I've got to get her," I told the others. "I love that dog!"

I took three long strides toward the beach, then a shrill cry shattered my focus.

"Nooooooo!"

Something grabbed my arm. I turned, wondering what in the world could possibly make a sound that blood-curdling, and to my horror I saw Daniel standing right behind me, his fingers clutching my sleeve, his mouth open and his eyes wide. "Don't go!" he yelled, his face reddening with effort.

Bewildered, I looked up at the others. They were all on their feet, staring at Daniel with confusion and bewilderment.

"Daniel?" Brenda flew down the stairs and fell to her knees in the sand. Her fingers fluttered over his head, his shoulders, his form as if she were afraid to touch him. "Are you okay?"

He closed his mouth and released my sleeve, then his eyes filled with tears. We waited, hoping he would speak again, but he simply lowered his head and trudged back up the steps and across the deck, then he went into the house.

Tank, the professor, Brenda, and I stared at each other, not knowing what to say.

Chapter 9

We left Brenda at the house with Daniel, who had gone into Sabba's den and curled up on the couch, burying his face in a pillow. Since he was either asleep or pretending to be, we figured it was best not to disturb him.

"I'll sit out here and watch TV or something," Brenda said, sitting in the living room. "If he needs me, I'll be here."

"Do you think he'll talk again?" Tank looked from Brenda to the professor. "He doesn't say much."

"Unless he wants to," I said.

"At times of great duress," the professor added.

I pressed my lips together and led the way back outside. I didn't understand what kind of duress Daniel and Abby had been under, but now that Daniel was safe, I had to find Abby. Most Labrador Retrievers are good swimmers and love the water, but Abby had been acting crazy when she took off. Plus, dogs weren't allowed on this beach, and I needed to find her before someone called Animal Control to pick her up.

The professor, Tank, and I spread out and walked south along the beach, stopping to ask people we met if they'd seen a chocolate Lab in or near the water. We got a lot of strange looks and head shakes, and one prim lady in a housecoat reminded me that dogs had their own beach Pinellas County and weren't supposed to share the sand with people. "Worms, you know," she said, sniffing. "And all these people walking around in bare feet."

I didn't have the heart to tell her that barefoot people stood a greater chance of stepping on glass or being stung by a stingray than getting worms from a dog, so I thanked her with a smile and kept walking. After about thirty minutes of beach-combing, I whistled, caught the professor's and Tank's attention, and pointed north. "Let's head back," I called. "She wouldn't have gone this far south."

As we moved north, Tank drifted from his center position and hobbled a few feet away from me. "I wouldn't worry about the dog," he said, obviously trying to ease my anxiety. "Labs are great swimmers. And dogs can find their way home pretty easily."

I looked over at him, grateful for his concern. "Thanks, Tank. I really appreciate your help, by the way. Not many people would agree to come out here and help me scour the beach, especially if they had a broken toe. The professor came only because I threatened to surprise him by translating his next speech into binary code."

"Shucks, Andi, I'm from a place where there ain't no beaches, so this is a treat for me. In fact—" he lowered his head so I couldn't see his face—"being with you is a treat, too. All week, most weeks, I'm with a bunch of rough, rude football players, and none of them can hold a candle to—well, none of them are much fun to be with after practice. So I'm glad you called. I'm glad I'm here."

He looked at me then, and in the golden glow of sunset I saw hope, happiness, and sincerity shining in his eyes. I'd seen that look in his eyes before, so maybe I realized what he was up to even before he did. If you took one innocent, good-hearted lug, added in a decent-looking girl of the right age, and multiplied the mood with mystery, danger, and a gorgeous sunset, you ended up with a guy who didn't know the first thing about having a girlfriend, but was awfully eager to learn.

I knew one sure way to nullify this equation before things got out of hand.

"Tank." I stopped and met his open gaze head on. "I appreciate you so much. I've never had a brother, so I think I'm going to like having you around."

I gave him a sweet smile, punched his rock of an upper arm, and strode toward the house, leaving him and the professor on the beach.

Chapter 10

"Dr. Mathis?"

We looked up from our pancakes when the professor raised his voice. His cell phone had rung during breakfast, and he hadn't bothered to leave the table.

I felt a tingle in my stomach as the professor listened to the marine biologist.

"Are you quite certain? Um-hmm. Nothing else could have done that? I mean—"

I grinned when the professor fell silent. Judging from the disgruntled look on the professor's face, Dr. Mathis was standing his ground.

"I see," the professor said. "Well, we appreciate the information."

He disconnected the call, slipped his phone back into his pocket, and picked up his knife and fork.

"Well?" I leaned toward him. "What did Mathis have to say?"

The professor began to cut his pancakes. "He necropsied the birds and fish last night. He could find no reason for the fishes' demise, so the man is obviously not very good at his job. Apparently your aquarium needs a more qualified marine biologist."

I bit back my impatience. "Professor! Is that all he said?"

Finally, he met my gaze. "Though he did not know what killed the fish or removed their eyes, he did determine that the birds died from blunt trauma. He believes the impact may have forced the eyes out of their sockets." He lowered his knife. "May I eat my breakfast now?"

I shifted my gaze to Brenda. "Blunt trauma? Like someone hit them?"

"Or they hit somethin'," Brenda said, thought working in her eyes. "Maybe they hit a jet."

I shook my head. "There were no jets overhead. Flights coming into Tampa International circle Tampa Bay, not this beach. Believe me, I've flown into Tampa enough times to know."

"It could have been a small plane," the professor said. "Any small plane could have been buzzing around and flown through a flock of birds. You have to admit, Andi, there's nothing strange about that. Airplanes and birds are always colliding in midair."

"A flock," I said. "A flock is what—twenty birds? A hundred? *Thousands* of birds fell on our beach, professor. I heard one of the guys from UT say there had to be at least ten thousand dead blackbirds. That's a big flock."

"Maybe they hit, like, a thunderhead." Tank lifted his orange juice. "That's up in the sky, isn't it?"

The professor opened his mouth, but I kicked him under the table, knowing he was about to remark on Tank's intelligence. The big guy couldn't help it if he spent more time in the locker room than in his books.

"A thunderhead," I explained gently, "is a cloud. It may be dark, it may have winds and lightning, but I don't think birds could kill themselves by running into one."

"So maybe this marine biologist guy is wrong," Brenda said. She poured two sugars in her coffee, then closed her eyes and breathed in the aroma. "Fresh ground coffee in the morning. I tell ya, I could get used to livin' like this. What do you think, Dan?"

I looked at the boy. He had gotten up to eat breakfast with the rest of us, but he kept glancing toward the sliding doors as if he expected to see Abby at any moment.

"I know, Daniel," I said. "I'm waiting for her, too."

"Did you check the SPCA?" Tank said. "Someone might have taken her to the lost and found."

"I'm going to call this morning. I'm also going to go out again and talk to people who live near the beach. She's such a nice dog, she'd have gone with anyone. But she's wearing a collar and tag, plus she's microchipped, so I'm hoping someone will call. I'm sure she'll turn up soon."

Brenda shrugged. "I hate to tell you this, but where I'm from? A good-sized dog like that would end up in the center of a fight pit as a bait dog. I have to say, though, last night your dog looked like she could give those fighting dogs a run for their money."

I stared at Brenda, horrified by the thought of Abby in a dog fight. I knew Florida had its share of such horrible crimes, but this was Pinellas County, home to thousands of retirees. None of our neighbors would be involved in something so despicable, but you never knew who might be strolling down a public beach.

"So . . ." I pushed away from the table and tapped my fingers on the edge. "We're stuck, huh? We don't know what killed the fish, we don't know what killed the birds, and we've lost Abby. This weekend is turning out to be an unmitigated disaster."

My cell phone jangled. I pulled it from my pocket and stared at the unfamiliar number, then pressed *receive*. "Hello?"

"Andi? Are you ready to give me your last name?"

I blinked, caught off guard by the question. But the voice evoked a distant memory, and suddenly it all came back: the white van on the beach. The hazmat guy.

"That all depends," I said, glancing at the professor. "Were you able to learn anything about why those animals died?"

"Do I get a name if I tell you?"

"You're already got my number," I reminded him. "So let me hear what you have to offer."

"The fish—unknown cause of death," he said. "The birds—COD is blunt trauma."

I closed my eyes. "So what caused the trauma?"

"I wish I could tell you, darlin'. But truth is, that's all I've got. That's all anybody's got right now."

I heaved a sigh. "Goldstein," I told him. "My name's Andrea Goldstein. And thanks for the answer."

I put my phone on the table and folded my hands. "Dr. Mathis's opinion was just confirmed by a guy from the University of Tampa's biology department. The birds died because they ran into something solid, and from the sheer number of dead birds we can surmise that the thing they ran into must have been huge. But there are no jets, wind turbines, or skyscrapers along this stretch of the beach."

"Okay, then." Tank slapped out a *ta-da-boom* on the table. "We have a confirmed fact. We're making progress."

Brenda snorted. "Dial it back, CSI. We got a big pile of nothin.'"

The professor lifted his coffee cup as if to say *touché*, but even though we had another piece of the puzzle, I had never felt farther from the truth.

"Andi, I appreciate your intellect, I am grateful for your technological assistance, and I admit you're pleasant company, but I simply cannot believe that you would ask us to go door to door like encyclopedia salesmen."

"Ease up, Professor," Brenda drawled. "The last encyclopedia salesmen died years ago. Nobody goes door to door anymore, especially in Florida." She turned to me. "Isn't this the state where people can shoot you if you knock on their doors without an invite?"

"No one's going to shoot you." I lifted my chin, struggling to overcome my rising irritation. "All I want you to do," I said for the fourth time, "is go up

63

and down the beach and ask people about two things: have they seen Abby, and did they see anything odd on the day of the fish and bird kill. Is that so hard?"

The professor grumbled under his breath, but he didn't speak again. Once he left the house, though, I knew he'd fill someone's ear with complaints.

So I'd have to go with him.

"Brenda—" I pointed south—"why don't you and Tank go that way? You can take Daniel with you. The professor and I will head north."

Disappointment filled Tank's face for an instant, but he smiled at Brenda and stood back as she and Daniel went down the stairs. The professor merely lifted his brows when I looked at him. "Ready?"

"You are a clever girl," he said, leading the way over the deck. "Pairing that lovesick boy with Brenda."

I nearly laughed aloud. "Tank is not lovesick," I said, grabbing an umbrella from the stand near the back door. "He's just infatuated or something."

The professor snorted. "Be careful, Andrea. Inside the biggest men reside some of the softest hearts."

"Did you make that up?"

"I would never write something so maudlin. I probably read it on a Hallmark card."

We walked the fifty or so yards to the closest house, then approached the back deck. All the beach houses in this area had welcome mats at the front and back doors, since residents spent so much time on the beach. The professor remained a good ten feet behind me, undoubtedly embarrassed by the possibility that someone might think he was some kind of solicitor. Dressed the way he was, in long pants and a tweed sport coat, complete with elbow patches, he *did* look like a guy who might be peddling Dyson vacuum cleaners.

"Hello?" I knocked on the screen door. "Anybody home?"

A moment later an older woman approached, a wide smile beneath her curious gaze. I searched my memory for her face, but she must have arrived after I left for college. "Hello?"

I introduced myself, said I was staying with my grandparents next door, and asked if she'd seen Abby. The woman was distressed to hear the dog was missing and promised to call if she spotted her.

"One more thing," I said. "Did you notice anything unusual the day the fish and birds died?"

The woman blinked rapidly. "They died right in front of us, isn't that unusual enough? I called 911 the day it happened, but they wouldn't send the police until we were practically suffocating from the stench."

"Did you see anything else unusual? Did you, for instance, see anything in the sky?"

The woman tilted her head, then opened the screen door and joined us on the deck. "I didn't see anything," she said, "because it was raining and I tend to stay inside when it's damp and cold outside. But my nephew was out here that morning, and he said he saw something. He sounded crazy, though, and then the birds and fish started dying so I forgot about what he said."

"Is your nephew around? I'd love to talk to him."

The woman's smile faded. "Of course he's around. He's unemployed, lazy, and he sleeps until three o'clock because he stays out drinking with his pals all night. He's around, all right." Her face brightened. "Want me to wake him?"

"He wouldn't mind?"

"Of course he'll mind. But I won't." She winked. "Just a minute, let me get the lazybones out of bed."

She went back inside the house, her slippers shuffling over the tile floor, and I turned to study the horizon. The professor stood facing the water, too, his arms folded, his eyes intent on the sky.

"I know what you're thinking," he said, his voice flat. "And you know it's preposterous."

"Nothing's preposterous, professor. What is it Sherlock Holmes always says? 'When you have eliminated the impossible, whatever remains, however improbable, must be the truth.'"

"You haven't ruled out a small plane, a weather balloon, and a fireworks display. Those birds could have run into any number of things within a few miles of this place. The storm gusts could have picked up their bodies and dropped them here. Stranger things have happened before."

"Yes, but let's hear what the nephew has to say."

A few moment later I heard the slap of bare feet on the tile, followed by the squeak of the screen door. "Yeah?"

I turned. The nephew—in his early thirties, stubbled, bed-headed, and wearing only a pair of cargo shorts—squinted at us, his round eyes bleary and bloodshot. On the side of his neck I saw a tattoo—a scorpion.

For a split second, the world seemed to sway on its axis, then I grabbed at the strings of reality and held them tightly.

"Sorry to disturb you," I said, knowing that the conversation would be significant, "but your aunt mentioned that you saw something odd the day of the mass fish and bird kills. Would you mind telling us what you saw?"

"Why? He leaned against the door frame and crossed his arms. "Nobody believes me."

"I'll believe you," I said, looking steadily into his eyes. "I've found myself believing a lot of unusual things lately."

He looked at me for a moment, then the corner of his mouth quirked in a smile. "It was early," he said. "I'd been out partying and I'd had a few drinks, if you know what I mean. I walked up to the house this way, 'cause I didn't want to wake Aunt Edna. The sun was just coming up behind the house, so I dropped into a chair to chill out for a minute. That's when I saw them."

"Who?"

"Balls of light. Orbs, I think they're called. Three of them were bouncing around near the waterline. It looked like they were playing tag or something, but they never went far, just in and out, up and down. Then one of them zoomed right up here and hovered next to the porch railing. I was more than a little freaked. I couldn't move, so I just sat there while it sort of hung in the air and studied me. Then suddenly, zip! It flew out over the water and disappeared. Its buddies went with it."

"Did you hear anything?"

"Don't think so. Maybe a little varooming sound, like the light sabers in Star Wars. Or maybe I just I *thought* I heard that. I don't know."

"How long did the orbs stay around? Five minutes? Ten?"

He shook his head. "I don't know. It was like time stood still, you know? When I shook myself out of my daze, the sun had come up and everything looked pretty normal, except for the rain. I thought I must have been dreaming or somethin', but when all those fish started washing up right after, I wondered if those orbs had anything to do with it."

"They were only balls of light?" I asked. "Nothing tangible? You didn't see metal or wood or vinyl?"

"Nothin' like that. Just light. But not mindless light, if you know what I mean. They knew what they were doin'. The one came over and studied me like I was some kind of specimen in a jar."

I slipped my hand into my pocket so he wouldn't notice that I had begun to tremble. "So they were autonomous."

"Yeah, whatever." He scratched absently at his chest, then looked at me. "You think they had anything to do with all that stuff dying?"

"I don't know. I wish I did." I nodded, then smiled. "Thank you."

"No problem." As the professor and I turned to walk away, he followed us to the edge of the porch. "Hey, if you need something to do tonight, we'll be gathering down at the corner bar. We got everything we need for a party—"

"Thanks!" I waved, then joined the professor on the beach.

Chapter 11

An afternoon shower sent all of us scrambling back to the house. "I thought Florida was supposed to be warm and sunny," Brenda groused.

"It is," I assured her, "but this is October, so you never know what you're going to get. It can be hot one day and cool the next—and it can rain almost any time."

After drying off, we went into the kitchen to make coffee and hot cocoa. I had to admit, the warmth of the liquid in my cup took the edge off the chill I'd felt ever since meeting Edna's nephew and hearing about what he saw on the beach.

The professor shared the nephew's story with the others. "But he was clearly drunk, and probably delusional," he finished, "so his story is not credible."

"I disagree," I countered. "He may have been drunk, but drunks still see things." I lifted a brow and lowered my voice. "With all due respect, Professor, you should know that."

The professor pressed his lips together, then looked over at Brenda and Tank. "I'm not sure what you've picked up, but you might as well know that I am a recovering alcoholic. And Andi is correct, of course. Drunks do see things. Sometimes they see things that are actually present."

"I would have believed him if he said the moon was made of green cheese," I said, then made a face. "Well, not really. But I knew he was going to tell us something important the minute he walked out on that deck."

"Because you noticed another pattern?" the professor said, softly mocking.

"Because I'd seen him before—on Brenda's Aquarium program."

Brenda sputtered into her coffee mug, then set it down and wiped her mouth with the back of her hand. "You're kidding."

"It was the same guy, down to the scorpion tat. You *saw* him."

Brenda didn't answer, but stared at her mug.

"The guy saw *orbs*?" Tank made a face. "Somebody better fill me in."

"Technically, an orb is a sphere," I said. "Lately the term has caught on with ghost hunters and UFO researchers. When they speak of an orb, they talking about a ball of light that moves independently and shouldn't be part of the scene."

"It's poppycock," the professor said, sipping his

coffee. "And those people are kooks. There's absolutely nothing scientific about their so-called investigations—it's all hocus pocus performed for television cameras or YouTube videos."

"I don't know." Brenda shook her head. "I've always had respect for people with mysterious gifts. A witch once worked a root on my aunt—sent Auntie to hospital until some church women came and prayed over her."

I made a face. "A *root*?"

"A spell." Brenda gave me a one-sided smile. "My world has mysteries, too. Some that science can't begin to explain."

"Actually," I said, leaning against the counter, "an alien craft *is* a logical explanation. It could emit heat or sound or some substance that poisoned that particular variety of fish. The birds could have run into the craft, suffering blunt trauma and dying from the impact."

"Maybe it didn't have to be big." Brenda frowned. "Maybe they were small but there were a lot of 'em, so that's why so many birds died." Her frown deepened. "That makes sense, though the thought of outer space creatures scares me spitless."

"Then why didn't anyone else see this improbable fleet of space ships?" the professor asked.

"A cloaking device." Brenda smiled and lifted a brow at Daniel. "Anyone who watches *Star Trek* knows about cloaking devices."

"Why didn't anyone *hear* this fleet?"

"It could have made sounds above or below the range of human hearing," I pointed out. "After all, dogs can hear things inaudible to the human ear—"

I froze as my thoughts crashed into a wall. *Abby*

heard it. The birds, the fish, the dogs heard everything. Ever since I'd arrived, Abby had been sitting by the sliding glass door, listening, watching, whining. But she ran off to chase some invisible something *after* the birds and fish died. So whatever had done the damage . . . was still around.å

Without saying another word, I set my mug on the table and walked to the wide glass doors. Gray clouds hung low over the sea, heavy with rain, and mists skirted the surface of the sand. Clouds were the perfect camouflage for anything . . . or anyone . . . that might be patrolling the earth.

Or spying on us.

In Port Avalon, the professor had made enemies who escaped. A man and a woman, he said, who had taken Daniel out of the hospital and worked with A.J. Van Epps to test the boy's supernatural abilities. We had good reason to believe the man and woman were affiliated with the Institute for Psychic Studies, which we'd pretty much trashed before we all found ourselves in Port Avalon . . .

I pressed my hand to the glass and peered past my reflection into the gathering darkness. Was Abby still out there? Were other things—aliens or spies—out there? Were they hovering nearby, maybe watching us now?

I startled when I heard the click of the latch on the door. I looked over and saw Daniel standing next to me, his gaze focused on something beyond the glass. Without speaking, he grabbed the handle, pulled the door open, and stepped into the storm.

What?

I turned to look at Brenda, but she and the others were already out of their seats and hurrying toward me. "Daniel," Brenda called softly, not wanting to frighten him. "Daniel, kid, come on outta the rain."

If he heard her, he gave no sign of it. Instead he walked forward, crossing the deck, stopping only when he reached the railing. For a moment I was afraid he'd continue down the stairs and make a run for the water as Abby had, but he stood motionless, his hands at his sides, as if he were waiting. For what?

"Never thought I was signin' on to be a babysitter," Brenda grumbled good-naturedly, but she went after the kid, ignoring the rain pelting her head and shoulders. "Danny, come on in before we catch a cold."

"He's not budging," I remarked to anyone listening. "I don't know what has mesmerized him, but he's not going to move."

"Let me take them an umbrella." Tank pulled one from the milk can and opened it, then crossed the deck in three giant hops. Like some kind of overgrown butler he held the umbrella over Daniel and Brenda.

"What are you all looking at?" I called through the open door, crossing my arms in a half-hearted effort to ward off the cold breeze. "What is Daniel looking at?"

"Something," Tank answered, an edge to his voice. "Something evil. I can feel it."

"There's *nothing* out there." Pushing his way through the space between my shoulder and the edge of the door, the professor went outside, too, and peered into the darkness. "There's nothing here," he yelled, glancing back at me. "Just sand, sea, and a pack of fools."

Then Tank tipped his head back and called out, his

voice loud enough for all of us to hear above the wind and rain: "Open our eyes."

Before I could draw another breath, the air between my friends and the beach seemed to shimmer, then a glowing shape filled the space. The shape was vaguely spherical, but the edges were soft and translucent. The outline glowed big and round like an odd golden moon, then it began to spin, slowly rotating until I saw an opening—a window?

I didn't realize I had walked onto the deck until I felt the splash of rain on my cheeks. A rough fabric brushed my elbow, and I knew the professor had joined me at the railing, all of us drawn forward by the object . . . or our own fascination. I opened my mouth to say something, but I couldn't speak. My lips were as dry as paper and my tongue as heavy as lead.

The opening—the window—shifted and shimmered, then a covering peeled back, like skin from an orange. From within the sphere, a form appeared—round, soft body, stick-thin neck, circular face. Long nose topped with a red rubber ball. Clown-like smile exaggerated and painted red beneath black eyes, with no white, no shine, no life at all.

Long fingers extended from a wrinkled hand and seemed to invite us closer, then one of the fingers waggled back and forth like a scolding schoolteacher's. The eyes blinked; the head turned. And then I heard a scream—not a human scream, but the sound of an anguished dog in pain.

Daniel's agonized howl mingled with my own. With my senses reeling and my gaze still fixed on the horrible caricature in the orb, I reached out for the touch of something—anything—solid, and caught Tank's arm. Beside me, Daniel stiffened, reached into the darkness, and collapsed.

The window closed, the orb spun and zipped toward the water, then it vanished.

Chapter 12

I closed my eyes as a scream clawed in my throat. That cry—surely that wasn't Abby. That couldn't be Abby. Why would anyone want to hurt her? She had never done anything but love me and my grandparents. She was the personification of love and faithfulness, so why would anyone—anything—want to hurt her?

This time Brenda couldn't stop herself. She ran forward and drew Daniel into her arms until he came to, then she kept holding him as he flailed, slapped at her head, and kicked her legs. The professor finally pulled Daniel away and helped him stand—alone in a corner, trembling and staring at nothing—until he could regain control of himself.

Brenda crumpled in a heap on the deck, burying her face in her hands as her shoulders shook with soundless sobs. Tank positioned himself in front of the steps in case Daniel decided to run down the beach, but after a few minutes the professor succeeded in persuading Daniel to go inside the house. The professor went with him, but I stayed on the deck, my hands gripping the railing, rain dripping from my nose and hair.

Tank held the umbrella over me, sheltering me from the percussive *plops* of fat raindrops. "Miss Andi," Tank said, his voice urgent, "what you saw out there—it can't hurt you. What we saw, what we heard—"

"The professor says we should only believe in what we can see and hear and touch," I answered, my voice shaking. "Well, I saw and heard, and I'll never forget it. We all saw and heard it—"

"Andi—" Tank hesitated. "There are more things in this world than you know."

A wry chuckle slipped from my lips. "This isn't the time to be paraphrasing Shakespeare."

"I'm not paraphrasin' anything," Tank replied. "But surely you know—I mean, look at us. Look at this group and think about the odds against us ever comin' together. We've been given special gifts, and I know there's a powerful reason for those gifts, just like I know there's a reason we've been brought together."

I pressed my hand to my head and turned toward the house. "I need to get inside. I need . . . light."

I made my way back to the kitchen, where the

professor handed me a clean towel. When he saw how my hands were trembling, he wrapped the towel around my shoulders, then went back to keep an eye on Daniel.

Tank stayed outside with Brenda, urging her to get up, even slipping his arm around her thin shoulders. I don't know how he did it, but he got her to come back inside, though the woman he escorted through the doorway looked nothing like the confident, sassy woman I'd come to know. Her eye was partly swollen—probably the result of a collision with Daniel's elbow—and her face was wet with tears and rain. Tank guided her to a chair, then handed her a clean towel as well.

"Let me turn on that fancy hot drink machine," he said, hobbling into the kitchen. "I think I can set us all up with coffee or somethin'."

A few minutes later, we were all sipping from hot mugs and sitting around the fireplace in the living room. Daniel lay in a huddle on Safta's bearskin rug, the professor had taken Sabba's easy chair, and Brenda perched on the edge of the oversized ottoman. I sat on the floor by the fire and watched as Tank finally took a seat next to Brenda. Only after a few minutes had passed did I realize that he had picked up a book on his way to the living room.

"I think—" my voice trembled—"we need to talk about what just happened. We need to compare notes from our varied perspectives."

"Nothing happened." The professor crossed his arms. "The boy had a breakdown, that's all."

I stared at the professor, but he refused to meet my gaze. Instead, he set his jaw and stared at the flickering fire.

I understood. His mind was still trying to sort through everything he'd endured in Port Avalon. Asking him to absorb all this, too—it was too much.

"I saw . . . an orb," I said, turning to Brenda and Tank. "For lack of a better word, I guess that's what I'll call it. It had a window, and I saw this . . . clown-like creature in it. And then I heard Abby scream."

Brenda, Tank, and the professor turned their heads sharply, looking at me with incredulity.

"You heard a dog?" Brenda said. "I heard a child."

"Sounded like a lineman to me," Tank said. "Like the guy I hit last season and broke his leg. I didn't mean to hurt him, but accidents happen. At least that's what Coach told me."

I looked at the professor and waited. Finally, after several seconds had ticked away on the mantel clock, he shook off his false indifference. "All right, I saw it," he said, his jaw tight. "I don't know what it was, but it was exactly like that young man described, so I have obviously been influenced by the power of suggestion."

"And what did you hear?" Brenda asked.

The professor clamped his lips together.

"Professor?" I tilted my head to meet his gaze. "We all heard something. What did you hear?"

A muscle worked in his jaw, then he glared at me. "I heard myself, okay? I heard myself screaming like someone had set me on fire. And while self-immolation is not something I aspire to, the experience was entirely too much like what I felt in the House in Port Avalon. So I do not wish to discuss it further."

"It's as if someone—" Brenda paused as if choosing the right word—"know us well. They're messing with our minds."

"If someone is messing with our minds," I said gently, "then who is that someone?"

Silence stretched between us as we considered the possibilities. We had seen strange forces at work in the past few weeks, and the fact that we kept finding ourselves together had persuaded us—or at least some of us—that someone kept bringing us together. If the uniting force was good, and the destructive force evil . . .

The professor would insist that life was rarely so black and white.

Tank broke the heavy silence by picking up his book. "Listen to this, guys: 'Therefore the land mourns, and everyone living there languishes, wild animals, too, and the birds in the air, even the fish in the sea are removed.'"

I looked at him, bewildered. "What are you reading?"

Tank shrugged. "I found this book on your grandfather's nightstand. I was flipping through it when I saw this bit about the birds and fish."

"Let me see that." I stood and went to Tank, then recognized the book. "You're reading from Hoshea. This is Sabba's copy of the Tanakh."

"Really." Cynicism lined the professor's voice. "Bad enough that we've all shared a mass hallucination due to the suggestions of the drunken fool next door, but to follow it all up with religious nonsense—"

"It's all here." Tank lifted the book. "The birds dying, animals, fish—it's all predicted here. The earth is mourning. The birds and fish and wild animals are dying, but no one wants to recognize the truth. Andi has seen the pattern, and she knows what it means."

"Tank." Brenda glared at him from beneath her dreadlocks. "What we saw out there had nothing to do with God."

"You're right about that." A small smile lit the big guy's face. "But what if God has an enemy, and his time is running out? He could be feelin' the pressure, and be determined to destroy as much as he can in the short time he has left. He's sent his minions out to destroy and confuse people—"

"That's it." The professor shook his hands as if washing them of everything we had seen and heard. "I'm going to bed. I'll see you all in the morning, when I expect we'll all be eager to get back on the jet and head home." He turned toward me. "Be sure to thank your grandparents, etcetera. This hasn't exactly been a relaxing time, but it has convinced me that I am as susceptible to mass hallucinations as anyone else."

One by one, they headed toward their rooms— Brenda and Daniel left after the professor, and soon only Tank and I remained by the fireplace. I missed Abby. The heaviness of grief was like a dead body strapped to my shoulders, weighing me down, draining my energy and my joy.

I knew Tank sensed my sadness. Anyone who knew me had to realize that if someone took Abby, they'd stolen something vital and precious from me.

"I . . . miss her," I said, my voice breaking. "I don't know if you can understand, but for years, she was the only friend I had. I was a misfit, but never around her."

Tank remained silent, letting my words hang in the space between us. And then, just when I thought he hadn't been paying attention, he reached out, caught my chin, and lifted my face to meet his gaze.

"God doesn't lie," he said simply, his gaze shifting toward the sliding doors as if that gruesome caricature of a clown might return at any moment. "And he's more powerful than anything out there."

"Then why," I asked, "couldn't he keep Abby safe?"

I got up and went to my room, too, leaving Tank alone to guard the fire.

Chapter 13

We ate breakfast—or Daniel did, anyway—in a thick silence. None of us wanted to talk about the night before, but every other topic felt silly and stupid in comparison. How could we talk about the weather or travel plans after what we'd seen? How could we talk about *anything*?

As shaken as we were, I didn't feel uncomfortable. For some reason, I felt weirdly connected to everyone at the table. Despite our differences and our disagreements, I knew I would rather be miserable with them than indifferent by myself.

Brenda made coffee, then filled four mugs and passed them out. Like automatons we poured in cream and sugars, then sipped and stared at the polished surface of the dining room table.

I never would have believed that Daniel would be the first to speak. "They were real," he said, making eye contact with me for the first time in—well, ever. "I see them all the time."

I blinked at him, then looked at the others, who were also watching Daniel. The boy didn't seem inclined to say anything else, though, and went back to eating his cereal.

"The kid is right, but I don't think they were aliens," Tank said. He spoke slowly, as if carefully considering each word. "I don't think that clown thing and his buddies came from another galaxy. They might have come from another dimension, and I'm pretty sure they've been on earth and around earth since the birth of this planet. I think they were demons, just like the ones we saw in action at the Institute for Psychic Studies."

I couldn't have been more surprised if Tank had begun to sing opera at the breakfast table. The big guy was usually two steps behind us, yet there he was, offering a theory that sort of made sense. But was it our answer?

"Demons?" Brenda looked at him with bleary eyes. "You're telling me I couldn't sleep last night because I saw a *demon*?"

Tank shrugged. "Fallen angels, demons—call 'em whatever you want. But they're real and they meddle in people's affairs . . . even though most sophisticated folks don't want to admit they exist."

"And that explains why you believe so devoutly," the professor said. He twisted in his chair. "So what's the point, Tank? What are we doing here? If these events are caused by supernatural forces, we mere humans may as well go home."

"No, because we have gifts. And we have power." Tank flashed a grin bright enough to be featured in a toothpaste commercial. "The power's not in us, but God can give us the power to fight them and the people who work for them. And more important, I think God's the one who brought us together. We're supposed to cooperate and warn people. We're supposed to interpret the signs."

"I didn't get a call from God," Brenda said, "I got a call from Andi. And God didn't fly me here, Andi's grandpa did. As I recall, you were on the same jet."

"Why did you come?" Tank asked quietly. "And don't tell me you came because you wanted a few days in Florida for vacation. I know better."

Brenda glared at him a minute, then looked at Daniel. "Don't matter why I came, and what happened yesterday don't matter, either. All that matters now is that we get Daniel back to—well, get him back for some help. This trip has stressed him out, and they're not gonna let me see him again if I don't take him back so he can get better."

"Wait." I looked around the table, frustrated that the others appeared to be giving up. "Aren't we going to investigate this further? We didn't solve anything. The animals—the planet—is still in danger."

Brenda set her coffee cup down. "Nothin' I can do about that. Like I said, I have to earn a livin'."

"I'm done here, too." The professor pushed back from the table. "My brain can only tolerate so much madness."

I waved my hand, about to suggest that talk some more, but a blur of movement outside the window distracted me. People on the beach were running toward something in the water.

My stomach tightened for no rational reason. Leaving the others at the table, I went to the sliding doors and stepped out, then ran down the stairs. From there I could see something tumbling in the wavewash, something dark, with straight legs like a table. Something brown, like *chocolate* . . .

I broke into a run.

By the time I heard someone shout, "It's a dog!" I was already approaching the water's edge. I splashed into the shallows and gripped Abby's collar, then pulled her onto the sand. Rigor mortis had already set in. Her legs were splayed straight out, as if she'd died in a standing position. Her brown eyes were missing, the empty sockets encrusted with sea salt.

I fell to my knees and balled my hands into tight fists, struggling against the sobs that welled in my chest. Soft murmurs from bystanders wrapped around me, and a moment later I heard the pounding feet of Daniel, Brenda, Tank, and the professor. They stood silently, watching me weep in the tide, then Daniel knelt beside me, too, bending to press his forehead to Abby's.

"Why did this happen to her?" I asked, glancing up at Tank. "You know who did it—and I heard her scream. They are evil, and they did this because they hate. I never understood hate until this minute, but I understand it now. They hate us, so they hurt and destroy and inflict pain on the ones we love . . ."

In a flash, I remembered how my grandparents spoke of the Nazis, and the people they knew who had lost mothers, fathers, siblings, and families in the Holocaust. Hatred, pure and simple and evil, had gripped Hitler and spurred him to blind his people with hostility and contempt. Whoever had tortured and killed Abby would do the same thing to a child, a family, anyone. That kind of hatred was elemental; it did not discriminate, but it loved to destroy innocence.

I lowered my head, too, and dared to place my hand on Daniel's shoulder. I needed to touch him, and in that moment I think he needed to be touched.

The bystanders peeled away, probably uncomfortable with our open grief. When we were finally alone, Tank knelt across from me and Daniel. I thought he was going to help me carry Abby's body up to the house, but instead he placed one hand on Abby's side and the other over her ravaged face.

A rush of gratitude flooded my heart. He was silently telling me that he understood, and he was sparing me the sight of her awful wounds.

I placed my hand on Abby's belly, next to Tank's. "It's okay," I whispered, my voice as ragged as my emotions. "If you'll help me carry her, we can find a spot to—"

I stopped, suddenly aware that the fur next to Tank's hand felt *warm*. His hand had reddened, and Abby's body seemed to grow warmer with every second. Tank's eyes remained closed, but I could feel *energy* flowing from his hands, over the dog, even tingling my fingertips—

Abby whined. I righted myself so suddenly that I fell on my butt in the wet sand. Daniel laughed as he buried his fingers in Abby's soggy fur, and Tank finally opened his eyes. He lifted his hands, releasing the dog, and Abby bounded up, then turned and shook herself off, her brown eyes sparkling above an enthusiastic grin.

I looked at the professor, who was speechless, probably for the first time in his life.

"Cowboy—" Brenda began, turning wide eyes upon Tank—"when did you become a superhero?"

Tank stood and brushed sand from his hands. "I dunno. Doesn't always work. But I figured that God wouldn't want the other to have the final word here, so I gave it a try."

He extended one of his healing hands toward me and helped me up, then gestured toward the house. "Guess we'd better go give that dog a bath."

Abby had not only been restored to me, but she seemed to have the energy and spunk of a pup. Tank and I knelt by Safta's huge bathtub as my girl splashed and alternated between trying to eat the soap bubbles and kissing our chins. I was exhausted by the time Tank hauled her out of the tub and toweled her dry.

I watched, amazed, as my rejuvenated Abby ran through the house, then sat prettily and offered her paw to everyone, even the professor.

Not once did she go to the window. Not once did I hear her growl.

We were in the living room when I finally gathered the courage to ask Daniel the question uppermost in my mind. "Abby saw the evil, too, didn't she?"

The boy slowly turned and met my gaze, then he nodded.

My heart thumped at the confirmation.

"And that evil—is it still out there?"

One corner of Daniel's mouth lifted in a small smile, then he shook his head.

I felt my shoulders relax. I could leave now,

knowing that Abby would be safe with Safta and Sabba.

"So what did we accomplish here?" Brenda asked, looking from me to the professor. "This wasn't much of a vacation."

"You got to see a dolphin show," Tank offered.

The professor snorted.

"I think—" I paused to gather my thoughts—"I don't think we did anything to that thing out there, but I think it did something to us."

Brenda made a face. "Speak for yourself. I'm fine."

"Not like that. I think it did something *in* us. We saw something horrible, and then we saw a miracle. The yin and yang, good and evil. And for now at least, the evil's gone and we're all here. Together."

The professor pressed his lips together, displaying his disagreement, but what could he say? He'd seen everything we'd seen, and he had no explanations for any of it.

"I'm done with that kind of crazy stuff. For now, anyway." Brenda stood and gestured to Daniel. "Let's go get your bag packed, okay? It's time to go home."

After Daniel stood and followed her, so did the professor and Tank.

I sighed and did the same.

Epilogue

Sabba and Safta arrived as we were packing. I gave my grandparents a hug, thanked them for their hospitality, and promised that I'd check in after I got back to my apartment.

"Did you have a good time with your friends?" Safta wanted to know.

"I don't think the word *good* really does it justice," I told her.

Before I left, I gave Abby a good brushing and thanked her for being so vigilant in her protection of us. "I see what you were doing," I whispered in her ear, "and I love you for it. Take good care of the folks, okay?"

We were lined up outside the house, waiting for the car Sabba had hired to take us to the airport, when a kid on a bike rode up and handed an envelope to Brenda. "For you," he said, then he grinned and rode off.

"Secret admirer?" Tank asked, winking at her.

Brenda snorted. "I'm not likely to find one in this neighborhood. This is probably a citation for trampin' through somebody's sea oats."

She took out the paper, read it, and frowned.

"What's it say?" I asked.

She shook her head. "This makes no sense to me, but maybe you guys can figure it out."

She handed me the paper, which I read aloud: "Likewise you, human being—I have appointed you as watchman. Yechizk'el."

I glanced at the back of the paper to see if I could find any clues as to who had sent it, but the page was blank.

"Forget it," the professor said, turning to search the road for any signs of our cab. "Someone's idea of a joke."

But it wasn't. With everything in me, I knew it was another piece of the puzzle.

FROM HARBINGERS 4
THE GIRL

ALTON GANSKY

From Chapter 1: Snow

Mr. Weldon pointed. "As you can see, Sheriff, these ain't Bigfoot tracks. If anything, they're Littlefoot tracks. If you catch my drift."

I stayed close to Uncle Bart and looked at what Mr. Weldon was pointing at.

A chill rose inside me. It didn't come from the snow, or the stiff breeze coming off the nearby mountains. This cold started inside my bones and clawed its way to the surface. No heavy coat can keep out a chill that starts on the inside.

Uncle Bart swore.

"Yep. My sentiments exactly," Mr. Weldon said. "You see now why I called so early?"

I'm not one of those people who frightens easily, and Lord knows I've seen some pretty chilling stuff over the last few months. During football season, I face some big guys. I'm big. Six-foot-three and a solid 260 but the guys I played against last season are bigger and meaner. There were several players on my University of Washington team that made me look small. Still, they don't frighten me. I like to think my faith has something to do with that, but this—

"Tell me what you see, Tank." Uncle Bart was testing me. For a moment I thought about giving a dumb answer, people are used to that, but this was too important. Besides, I didn't like the idea of trying to fool Uncle Bart. "Stop thinkin', boy, give me your first impressions."

"It's a footprint." I raised a hand. "I know, that part is obvious." It took me a moment to get the words to flow. "It's no animal. It's a human print. Small and—" The next part was difficult to say. "I can see toe prints."

"What does that mean to you, son?" Uncle Bart raised his gaze to me. Maybe it was my imagination but he looked almost as white as the snow on the ground.

"They're the footprints of a child. A child without shoes." I inhaled a lungful of cold air. "Uncle Bart. The kid is going to freeze his feet off."

"Or *her* feet."

Uncle Bart's words were a punch to my gut.

SELECTED BOOKS BY ANGELA HUNT

Roanoke
Jamestown
Hartford
Rehoboth
Charles Towne
Magdalene
The Novelist
Uncharted
The Awakening
The Debt
The Elevator
The Face
Let Darkness Come
Unspoken
The Justice
The Note
The Immortal
The Truth Teller
The Silver Sword

The Golden Cross
The Velvet Shadow
The Emerald Isle
Dreamers
Brothers
Journey
Doesn't She Look Natural?
She Always Wore Red
She's In a Better Place
Five Miles South of Peculiar
The Fine Art of Insincerity
The Offering
Esther: Royal Beauty
Bathsheba: Reluctant Beauty

Web page: www.angelahuntbooks.com

Facebook: https://www.facebook.com/angela.e.hunt

Don't miss the other books in the Harbingers series:

The Girl, by Alton Gansky.

The Call, by Bill Myers

The Haunted, by Frank Peretti.

52729847R00058

Made in the USA
Charleston, SC
24 February 2016